DETROIT PUBLIC LIBRARY
3 5674 03008449 6

W9-BXS-610

Phantom of the Prairie

Year of the Black-footed Ferret

by Jonathan London

Illustrated by Barbara Bash

Sierra Club Books for Children
San Francisco

For Bitsy Heckert & wildlife pros Roland Smith & Tom Thorne, with thanks — JL

To that place of alertness and wildness in us all — BB

The Sierra Club, founded in 1892 by John Muir, has devoted itself to the study and protection of the earth's scenic and ecological resources — mountains, wetlands, woodlands, wild shores and rivers, deserts and plains. The publishing program of the Sierra Club offers books to the public as a nonprofit educational service in the hope that they may enlarge the public's understanding of the Club's basic concerns. The point of view expressed in each book, however, does not necessarily represent that of the Club. The Sierra Club has some sixty chapters in the United States and Canada. For information about how you may participate in its programs to preserve wilderness and the quality of life, please address inquiries to Sierra Club, 85 Second Street, San Francisco, CA 94105, or visit our website at www.sierraclub.org.

First Edition

Library of Congress Cataloging-in-Publication Data
London, Jonathan, 1947 –
Phantom of the prairie: year of the black-footed ferret / written by Jonathan London; illustrated by Barbara Bash.
p. cm.
"A Sierra Club book."
Summary: When Phantom, the quickest ferret of the litter, pokes her head up and springs out of the tunnel, she begins her sometimes dangerous, always adventurous life on the prairie.
ISBN 0-87156-387-8 (alk. paper)
1. Black-footed ferret — Juvenile fiction. [1. Black-footed ferret — Fiction. 2. Ferret — Fiction.] I. Bash, Barbara, ill. II. Title.
PZ10.3.L8534Ph 1997
[E] — dc21 96-51149

Acknowledgment The author extends special thanks to Tom Thorne, black-footed ferret specialist, for his generous gift of time, energy, and knowledge.

Printed in China
10 9 8 7 6 5 4 3 2 1

Author's note Black-footed ferrets are the rarest mammals in North America. In fact, by the late 1970s, these elusive relatives of otters, skunks, weasels, and wolverines were believed to be extinct. Then, in 1981, a group of black-footed ferrets was discovered in a prairie dog town near Meeteetse, Wyoming.

Tragedy struck in 1985, when disease killed all but eighteen of the ferrets. The remaining animals were taken into captivity and a breeding program was begun. Happily, that program has been successful, and black-footed ferrets have been reintroduced into the wild in Wyoming, South Dakota, Montana, and Arizona.

Black-footed ferrets became endangered because humans tried to wipe out their principal prey, prairie dogs, which were believed to compete with cattle for grass. Only by supporting the Endangered Species Act, which protects black-footed ferrets and their prey in designated prairie dog towns, can we ever hope to glimpse these mysterious, masked "phantoms" of the prairie.

— Jonathan London

It’s spring on the high prairie,
and yip-yapping prairie dogs
pop up among the Indian paintbrush
and wild iris.

Beneath the rolling waves of grass,
four black-footed ferret kits
quietly drink their mother's milk.

Born with eyes shut tight,
they curl in a burrow
abandoned by a prairie dog
and sleep the day away.

In summer, thunder rumbles
and the air is filled
with the songs of larks
and red-winged blackbirds.
The kits are half-grown now,
furry and frisky,
wiggling with excitement.

One night, Phantom — quickest of the litter —
pokes her head up, looks around,
and springs out of the tunnel,
followed by the others.

While the prairie dogs sleep
deep in their burrows,
the ferret kits play.
Phantom walks on her tiptoes,
jumps, nips her mother's nose . . .
and is first to bound after her
in single file.
Soon the kits are stalking
grasshoppers and deer mice,
bouncing nimbly
through the tall grass.

Quiet as the moonlight,
Phantom creeps toward a flower,
crouches, stares . . .
and pounces!

But the ferrets
aren't the only ones
who stalk.
Behind some sagebrush,
Coyote crawls silently
on his belly . . .

and pounces —
catching the smallest kit.
Next time, Phantom
will be more watchful.

All through summer,
the kits learn to hunt
prairie dogs, their favorite prey.
And by the time the cottonwoods
down along the creeks
flare yellow with autumn,
Phantom is ready to search
for her own prairie dog town.

She sniffs and scampers
over low hills, through deep grass,
straying farther from the others.
Until one evening, over a rise she spies
the last prairie dogs of the day
as they yip and waddle down their holes,
their cheeks stuffed
with grass and seeds.

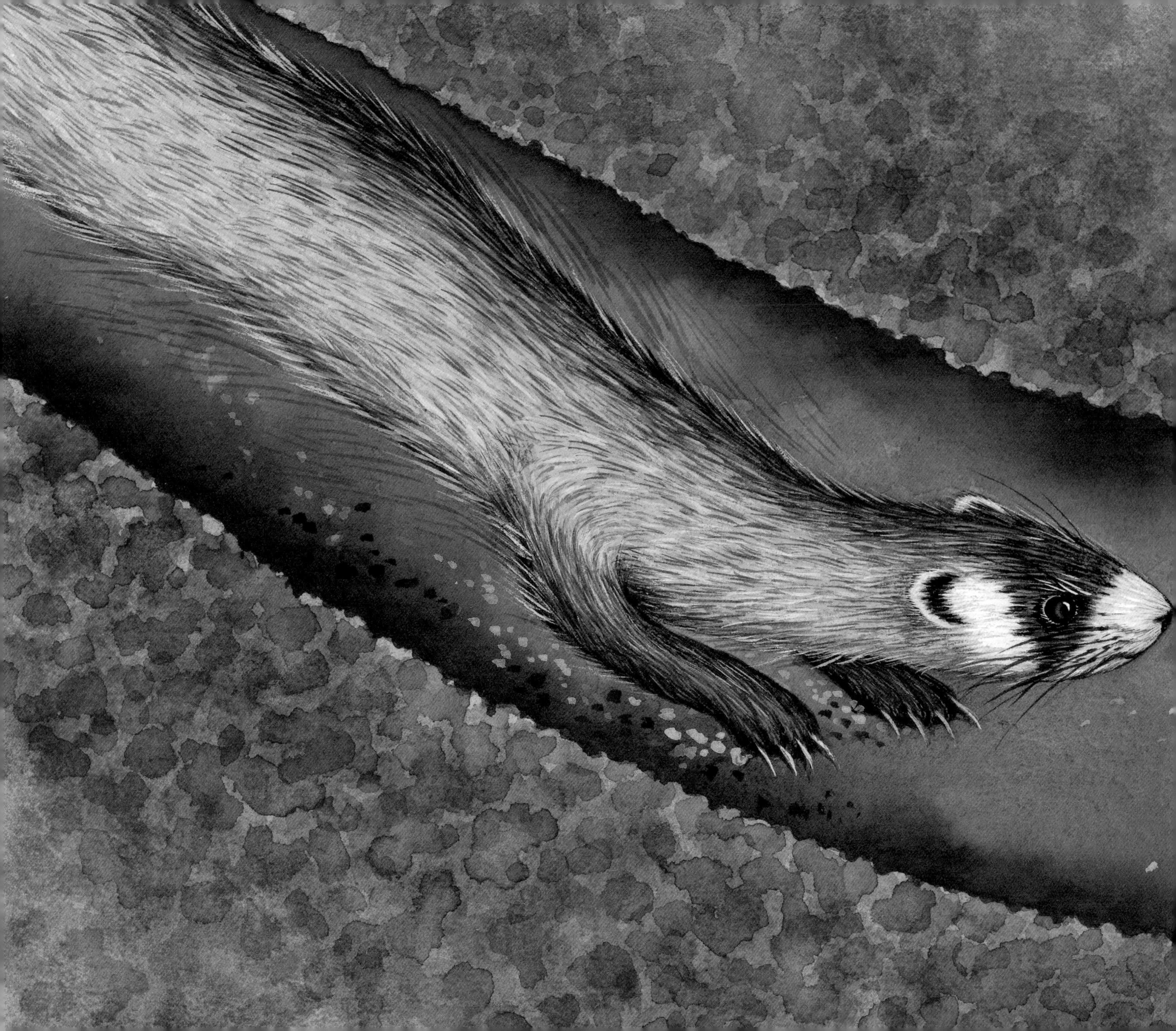

Hungry, Phantom claws
at the mouth of a tunnel plugged with dirt,
then backs out, again and again,
a load of earth against her chest.
Sleek, snake-like, she slithers
into the prairie dog's burrow.
And after a furious chase, Phantom —
faster and stronger — drags her prey away.

Winter comes on the wind
off the mountains
and blows the first snow
across dog town.

When the cottonwoods crack with frost,
the prairie dogs sleep more and more,
deep beneath the snow.

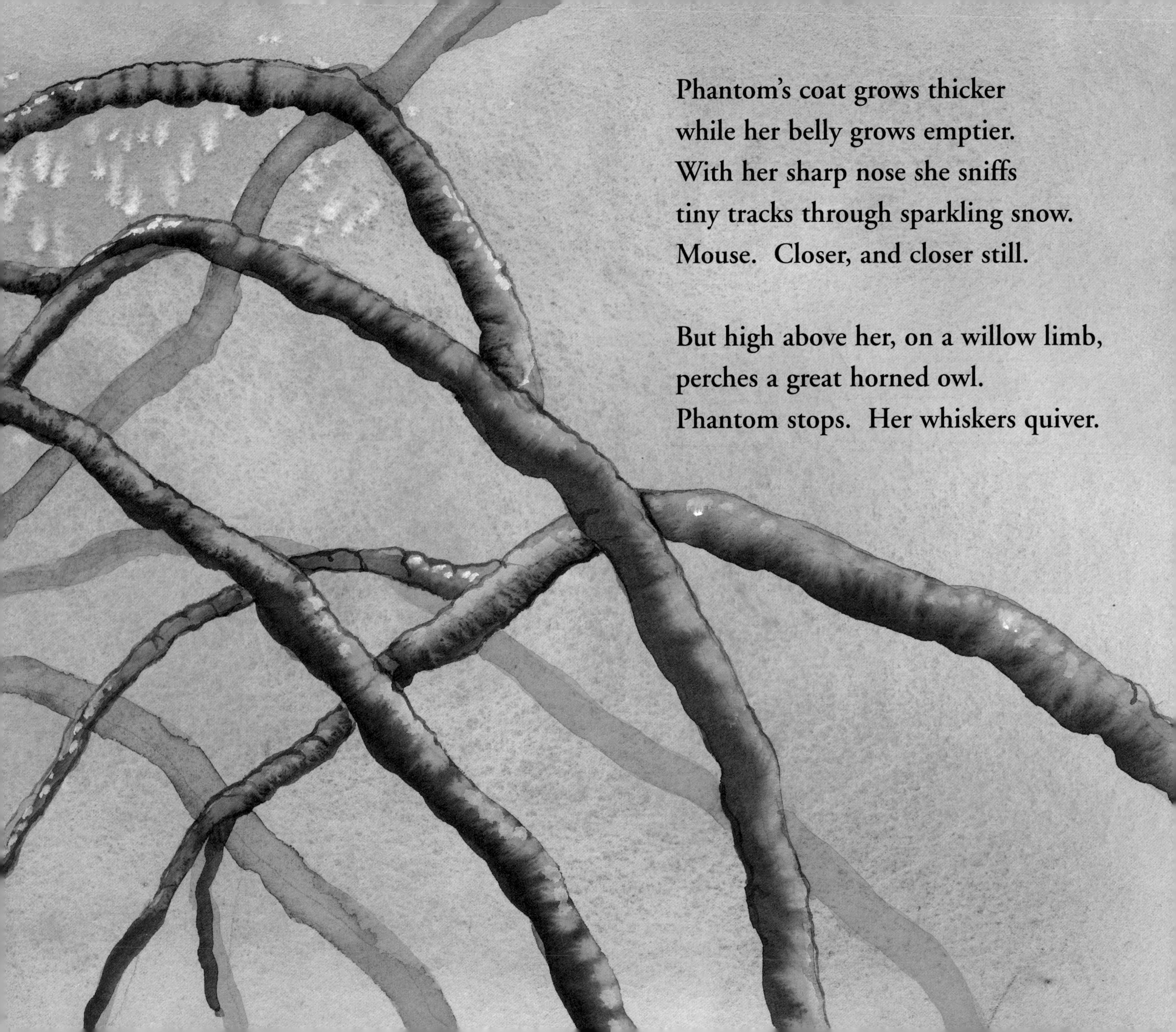

Phantom's coat grows thicker
while her belly grows emptier.
With her sharp nose she sniffs
tiny tracks through sparkling snow.
Mouse. Closer, and closer still.

But high above her, on a willow limb,
perches a great horned owl.
Phantom stops. Her whiskers quiver.

In a thicket, crouches her old enemy,
Coyote. In the bright light
of the full moon,
Phantom's quick black eyes
flash emerald green —

and she is gone,
as if the wind-swept snow
has swallowed her.
Coyote's pounce is too late.
Phantom has slipped down a tunnel
and shivers in safety.

At last, spring leaps on the high prairie,
and dog town bursts with life.

One night, beneath the stars,
Phantom bounds gracefully
from mound to mound
on springy, black-stockinged feet.

She stops,
stands up thin and tall,
and sniffs the air.
Something slinks
in the sagebrush.

Another black-footed ferret!
Frisky Phantom spins and dances,
looping high above the flowers.
She and the long, sleek male
will mate.
Then she'll be
alone again.

But not for long.
Six weeks later,
beneath the rolling waves of grass,
four black-footed ferret kits
quietly drink their mother's milk.